HONORIS VIRILIS RESPECTU

A SECURITY DIRECTORATE SHORT STORY

ALEXANDRIA BLAELOCK

Also by Alexandria Blaelock

HONORIS VIRILIS RESPECTU

A SECURITY DIRECTORATE SHORT STORY

ALEXANDRIA BLAELOCK

BlueMere Books
MELBOURNE, AUSTRALIA

For permission requests, please contact
enquiries@bluemerebooks.com.

Ordering Information:
Discounts are available on quantity purchases. For details, contact orders@bluemerebooks.com.

Honoris Virilis Respectu/Alexandria Blaelock
paperback ISBN: 978-1-922744-82-1
digital ISBN: 978-1-922744-83-8

Book Layout © BookDesignTemplates.com
Cover Art © i.am.norton33@gmail.com/Depositphotos

HONORIS VIRILIS
RESPECTU

Major General John Simm stood at his office window looking down and out over the City.

It was a beautiful day; the sun was shining, and the glass radiated a slight warmth back to him.

Were he a fanciful man who believed in a beneficent universe, he might have believed the small touch of warmth on his face, against the air-conditioned chill at his back was a small blessing.

Or perhaps a token of gratitude for his efforts.

But he was a Security Directorate Officer.

A Eugenics Programme success, he'd passed the Genomics Bureau post-natal testing, survived the State Academy of Cultural Regulation with a useful genetic "superpower" and graduated with Honours from the University of Civilisation.

Into a career he'd more or less been bred and trained for.

Out in the City, people the size of ants walked the streets in their shirt sleeves. Uniform jackets cast aside or held by a crooked finger over the shoulder, and uniform caps set at jaunty angles on heads.

It seemed joy strolled the streets with the citizens.

Something in the sunshine gave them the hope all was well in their universe.

And it was Simm's job to make sure they believed it was.

Because if they believed all was well, then it was.

He decided where the truth lay and oversaw the teams crafting the key messages to go out in the news feed.

That his office was so high above the population was symbolic, of course; given his high rank in the Propaganda Bureau, he needed to be seen to be above the common people.

To be surrounded by untainted empty space to exercise the appropriate level of "impartial" judgement.

Not for the first time, he wished he worked in an older building, with windows that opened so he could, now and again, let fresh ideas in with the fresh air.

All this streamlined modern efficiency wasn't very helpful for choosing a way forward, regulation twenty square metre glass office or not.

He sighed and returned to the black leather chair behind his overly large mahogany desk, boot heels clicking across the white marble floor.

The desk had its back to an impressively plain mahogany bookshelf packed with red leather-bound books and campaign awards.

A green pot plant on the top added a touch of life and colour as it spilled down the side.

He sprawled as much as his rank and training would allow.

And looked past the two black leather guest chairs in front of his desk, and the matching mahogany and leather conversational setting between them and the door.

Staring at the large picture of the Director General watching over him, dominating the view from his desk.

Just in case he forgot who was really in charge of the truth.

All had been well in his universe until a few weeks ago.

Captain Evans was bringing coffee in for him and his department heads when she'd slipped on the recently refinished floor and broken her hip.

He hadn't realised how dependent on her he'd become until she was gone.

The surgery was successful, but he'd be without her for months while she undertook physical therapy.

Her attitude had been so positive he'd chosen to watch out for her. Ensure her medical needs were taken care of, and guaranteed her position within the Directorate.

But he was already facing pressure to replace her.

And it was possible she wouldn't recover her full mobility, and even though she had a desk job, this put her career in jeopardy.

No one wants to be confronted by officers wounded in the line of duty.

Not to mention, no matter how successful the recovery, she wouldn't be combat-ready for active service ever again.

In a completely random stroke of good fortune, Captain Evans was the first assistant allocated to him on his promotion to the post years ago.

Aside from being an excellent administrator, she knew a lot about him and his executive team, and he could safely rely on her to adequately progress issues on his behalf.

While she hadn't passed sufficient units to graduate from the University of Civilisation, her underprivileged background had given her street smarts in spades, and she'd been able to talk her way out of the Protection Squad and into an administrative career.

And given him good advice when he'd tested ideas on her.

Then again, maybe street smarts was the genetic "superpower" that got her through the Academy and into University.

And a field promotion to officer-status.

Not that you were permitted to discuss or compare your powers.

But hers had made her sufficiently useful, and she was allocated to him on that basis.

Plus, her cheerful disposition was a ray of sunshine in itself, making friends and allies of all she came into contact with.

Not to mention her solid work ethic had gained the respect of his colleagues and direct reports.

Or that she was a keen judge of character, and had saved his arse on more than one occasion.

Her replacement, Lieutenant Smythe, had graduated, and that was the very best you could say about him. The worst was he was perhaps so thoroughly indoctrinated he didn't seem to have a single unauthorised thought in his head.

He couldn't rely on the boy to anticipate anything, or take the initiative to progress the slightest of issues without the most detailed of explicit instructions.

Not to mention Smythe's attitude clearly communicated his disdain for the posting and his belief he deserved something better. Thus he'd taken next to no time alienating Simm's colleagues and direct reports as thoroughly as Evans had charmed them.

The brat couldn't even make a decent cup of coffee.

The only thing he had in his favour were high-ranking parents, and they could only get him so far in the face of his incompetence.

The sooner Simm was shot of him, the better.

The day Evans slipped was the day he'd quietly started questioning the propaganda, and his place in the myth-making department of the Directorate.

Every day, he swore his loyalty to the Director General, the same as every other day since he started at the Academy.

But it was becoming clear to him that his idea of what the Security Directorate was, and the current Director General's idea were not the same.

Obviously, the communications equated them quite closely, but the Directorate existed outside the person who held the position of Director General.

A concept the current incumbent did not seem to grasp.

Or want to.

Simm was beginning to understand why there had been several attempts made on the figurehead's life.

Though, of course, the main way the DG acceded to the position was through a series of strategic assassinations, so it was only fair that other ambitious officers did the same.

But the politics of the situation were getting out of hand, and he realised that the time was coming when he would have to take a side - the Directorate, or its current leader.

Or more realistically, the current DG, and however many challengers there were.

And the only person he could talk to about his concerns was in a care facility undertaking intensive physical therapy.

The medics had barely removed her from his office when all the little niggles had started rising to the surface.

Smythe had arrived unannounced, and the first thing he'd done was throw her personal possessions in the bin.

Not reported for duty.

Not handed over his orders.

Not even acknowledged his new boss.

Simm had gone out to ask one of her colleagues to step in, and found the boy making himself at home at her desk when he got back.

The boy's barely concealed contempt for his new boss made him wonder what the Smythes senior had said about him.

Not that it mattered.

Simm was determined to get rid of him, and get Evans back as soon as possible.

It was her plant decorating his bookshelf, and after some sharp words to the boy, he'd taken the rest of her things and kept them in an archive box in his office.

Perhaps he was too sharp, and perhaps if the boy had followed protocol and reported in first, they might have got off to a better start.

But Simm's gut feel was the boy was a spy reporting back to someone else, who was intent on replacing him as Director of the Propaganda Bureau.

That he was about to find himself with a different, less important job, in a different department in a district far, far away.

Or perhaps a casualty of someone else's tilt for the leadership.

Maybe he needed to get out to that care facility and see what Evans knew.

Preferably before the boy ballsed up anything important.

Stuck in rehab or not, she always had her finger on the pulse, and today felt like a good day for a sitrep.

He stood and paced up and down his office, ostensibly thinking deeply, but really waiting for the boy to absent himself for long enough to permit a clean getaway.

He wondered whether to lock up his files, but reasoned that one way or another, the boy already knew the gist of most of it. And he probably couldn't cock anything else up any further than he already had.

Though it was uncertain whether Simm could recover his reputation.

After a point, the boy left, and Simm sloped out of the office and into the stairwell. Ran down several flights, crossed to the other side of the building and caught a lift to the basement carpool.

At the counter, he signed the appropriate requisitions for a car and driver and was soon in a black executive vehicle on his way.

The driver cleared his throat, and when Simm looked at him, he asked, "You're January Evans' commanding officer?"

Simm nodded.

"Is she doing well?"

"So far, so good."

"If you don't mind me asking Sir, do you know anything of the circumstances of the incident?"

"She slipped on the resurfaced floor."

The driver frowned, "may I speak freely Sir?"

Simm narrowed his eyes slightly, assessing the driver, then nodded his assent.

"There are rumours in the lower ranks it wasn't an accident, and she wasn't the intended target."

The driver glanced at him in the rear-view mirror before looking back at the road.

Simm considered the news.

Not out of line with what he'd been thinking, but the attack, if it was an attack on him, came sooner than expected.

"Do the rumours have any other information to add?"

"You might want to keep an eye on Smythe."

That goddamned boy.

Simm frowned, also in keeping with his thoughts.

"Thank you driver."

Not much later, they passed through the gates of the rehabilitation hospital.

The driver got out of the car, opened the door, and saluted as Simm climbed out. "Would you like me to wait Sir?"

Simm smiled slightly, "if you're prepared to be my alibi, you may wait in the mess hall Private..."

"Langley Sir."

"I'll call for you when I'm ready to leave Langley."

"Uh, Sir?"

"Yes Private."

"Please pass my best wishes on to Captain Evans Sir."

Simm nodded and returned the salute before turning and jogging up the stairs and through the hospital doors.

Her room was empty, and an attendant directed him to the loggia.

The loggia was an outdoor area within the ground floor footprint of the main building, like a room that was missing three walls.

Patients with various levels of ability and assistance were walking up and down.

Others, like Evans, were sitting, or lying, around the edges, looking out over a garden and across the City in the distance.

More sat at tables on the lawn or walking along paths between the garden beds.

Evans saw him coming and rose to salute.

He saluted in return and gestured for her to sit.

She shook her head slightly, picked up a cane, and took a few steps out to the lawn.

He rushed to catch up and take her arm.

Evans stiffened for a moment but allowed herself to relax and lean into him, gesturing to a table with her cane.

He nodded, "how is the rehab coming along?"

"I'm tired and sore, but the doctor says I'm fit for light duties."

"That's great news, but do you have any idea what they think light duties are?"

She laughed, "not yet, though I expect it'll all be listed out on the Return to Service orders."

"Then I shall have to see what they recommend and work out how I can make it easy for you."

He pulled a chair out for her, and she sat, "thank you Sir, I appreciate that."

He dragged another chair closer, and arranged it so they were facing each other, and between them, had an excellent view of all approaches.

He scanned the surroundings, "I heard that your accident may not have been an accident and that you may not have been the target."

She looked passed him as she replied, "yes, I've heard that too. Who told you?"

"Private Langley. He seems a little sweet on you."

"Langley, Langley, Langley... Motor pool Langley?"

"Yes, that's the one."

"Ah. He's a credible source. Did he say anything else?"

"When he dropped me off, he asked me to pass his best wishes on to you."

"Is he waiting for you?"

Simm nodded.

"Right. Do you think you could send for him so I can speak with him while you query my Return to Service orders?"

"Naaaww. Are you sweet on him too?"

"Oh, for god's sake, did you not just hear me say he was a credible source? The comms lines are monitored, so we need to speak face to face where they can't overhear us."

Simm cleared his throat, "oh. I see. Uh, I expect you'd like me to do that now?"

"If it's not too much trouble Sir."

"How much time do you need?"

"At least 15 minutes."

Simm looked at his watch, "shouldn't be too hard."

He walked back to the loggia and asked one of the attending therapists to send for his driver and page the doctor.

And before too long, he was in an untidy office discussing Evans' return conditions.

She was doing well, and they could discharge her today as long as there was someone to help her out at home.

And no, barracks didn't count.

She needed to maximise her movement and limit her sitting; starting at half an hour at a time and working up.

She'd need a cane for a few months. It would limit her ability to carry things.

She'd be on pain medication and would need to continue her rehabilitation for perhaps as long as six months.

She'd be tired until she built up some stamina and endurance. She should start her return with half-days, working up to full days over the next few weeks.

But she must be careful not to overdo it, or she'd find herself back in residential rehab.

It was all manageable within the scope of her duties. Even at half-time, she was more efficient than the boy, though according to Langley, there was more going on there than met the eye.

With Return to Service orders, her potentially useful superpower, and his right to choose his assistant, his prospects for getting her back were better than ordinary.

Simm didn't see any obstacles, but it remained to be seen what Langley might bring to their attention.

With a spring in his step, he returned to Evans.

Langley stood, saluted, then turned and walked a few paces away. He was still within earshot, but back to them, looked as though he was admiring the view of the City.

"All good," Simm said, "if there's someone to care for you at home, you can leave today and return to your duties tomorrow."

Evans stood and gave her hip a soothing rub.

"Right, that's good news. It seems we don't have much time."

"Much time?"

"I can't tell you more than that. Their plans are in progress, and we can't have you giving the game away."

"The game?"

"Yes John."

And Simm wondered for a moment if he'd already picked a side.

And whether it was the right one.

But Evans was an excellent assistant - and she'd said and done nothing to make him suspect her. There were no obvious reasons to distrust her now.

"Are you going to be all right?"

"Yes. You just need to act normal for a week or so while we," she gestured at Langley's back, "get this sorted out."

"Are you going to be all right?"

She laughed, "of course Sir. All those associations and cliques and so on are not what they seem."

"You're not really an assistant are you Evans?"

"No Sir, I'm not. But I can't tell you what I am."

"Of course not.

"But after this incident?"

"Well, let's wait and see."

Langley helped him get her packed and into the car. They dropped her back at her apartment. The one Simm knew she lived alone in.

She assured him she'd be fine. She'd be taken care of.

The drive back to the office was a quiet one. There was so much he wanted to know, but he didn't know where to start.

Assuming he had the clearance to know.

And in any case, he doubted Langley would give him answers.

How could Evans not be an assistant? She'd worked for him for years, and he'd had no idea she was anything more than an exceptionally bright young woman.

Had she qualified at University and gone deep undercover?

Was she even injured?

He struggled to get through the week.

He expected goons with guns to break in at any moment. Or some kind of enormous announcement on the news feed.

But there was nothing.

If anything, each day was more ordinary than the last.

The meetings were even more tedious, the boy even more incompetent, even more paperwork piling up in his tray.

At every turn, he hit a blank, featureless wall of ordinariness.

By the time Monday came around again, he was at peak restlessness, so when he saw Evans at her desk, he was unusually effusive in his greeting.

She followed him into his office, leaning on a cane with one hand, carrying a notebook in the other.

He opened his mouth to question her, but she cut him off.

"I can't tell you anything," she said, "you don't have the clearance."

"I beg your pardon? What do you mean I don't have clearance?"

"It's an operational matter Sir."

He grunted, "operational matter."

"Yes Sir, outside your purview."

"But if it was about me, surely I deserve to know."

"I can't possibly comment."

He sat behind his desk and waved at the chairs in front of it.

Smiling, she sat down and leaned her cane against the desk.

"And what about you Evans?"

"Clean bill of health Sir,"

"That's not what I meant, and you know it."

"Well, I'd like my plant back Sir."

"You're staying?"

"Yes Sir. I'm staying."

"Oh, thank goodness."

He didn't know what her job really was, but she was an excellent assistant, and he was glad to have her back.

THE END

ABOUT THE AUTHOR

Alexandria Blaelock writes stories, some of them for *Ellery Queen's Mystery Magazine* and *Pulphouse Fiction Magazine.*

She's also written five selfhelp books applying business techniques to personal matters like getting dressed, cleaning house, and feeding your friends.

She lives in a forest because she enjoys birdsong, and the smell of gum leaves. When not telecommuting to parallel universes from her Melbourne based imagination, she watches K-dramas, talks to animals, and drinks Campari. At the same time.
Discover more at www.alexandriablaelock.com.

IF YOU ENJOYED THIS STORY...

try the other Security Directorate stories

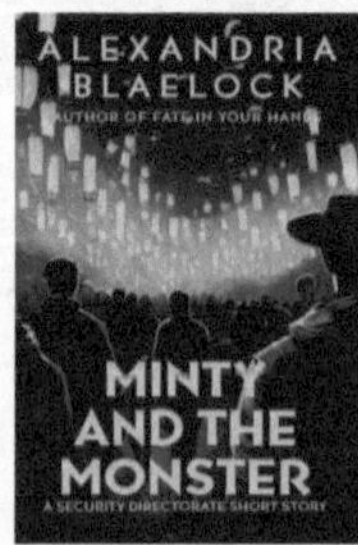